Say You Love Me

Dave Sargent is a lifelong resident of the small town of Prairie Grove, Arkansas. A fourth-generation dairy farmer, Dave began writing in early December, 1990. He enjoys the outdoors and has a real love for birds and animals.

Say You Love Me

By

Dave Sargent

Illustrated by

Jane Lenoir

Ozark Publishing, Inc.
P.O. Box 228
Prairie Grove, AR 72753

Library of Congress in publication data
F
Sargent, Dave, 1941-
Say you love me / by Dave Sargent; illustrated
by Jane Lenoir
Prairie Grove, AR : Ozark Pub., 1998
p.cm.
PZ7-S2465Say 1998
{Fic}21
1567631290 cloth
1567631304 (pbk. : alk. paper)
A son comes to realized how much his mother has
always loved him only when he is grown up.
Mothers and sons --Fiction.
Lenoir, Jane, 1950- ill.
4504931

Ozark Publishing, Inc.
P.O. Box 228
Prairie Grove, AR 72753
1-800-321-5671

Printed in the United States of America

Dedicated to

every mother in the world.

Foreword

A boy realizes the depth of his mother's love when it is too late.

Say You Love Me

If you would like to have the author of the Bird Pride Series visit your school, free of charge, just call 1-800-321-5671 or 1-800-960-3876.

When Billy was six years old, his father left for work one morning and never returned.

Billy's mother now had to provide for their every need. There was little time for anything but work.

When Billy was in the third grade, his class planned a field trip to the zoo.

They were going to eat lunch at McDonalds, and everyone was to bring three dollars.

Billy was very excited about
the trip and couldn't wait to get
home and tell his mother all
about it.

When Billy told her about
the trip and she read the note, she
felt sad. She didn't have an extra
three dollars.

That night when Billy fell asleep his mother sat at the kitchen table and thought, "If I buy oatmeal this week instead of Billy's favorite cereal, I could save sixty cents, and if I walk six blocks to the bus stop and ride

the bus to work instead of driving, I could save one dollar and eighty cents. Then if we have beans again on Friday instead of meatloaf, I could save eighty cents."

Billy went with his class to the zoo, and they all ate at McDonalds and had a lot of fun.

A few years later when Billy was in the tenth grade, he was on the football team.

All the football players were
going to get jackets with their
names on them. The jackets cost
sixty dollars each.

When Billy told his mother about the jacket, she felt bad, for sixty dollars was more than she had.

That Saturday she started looking for some part-time work to make the sixty dollars.

The only work she could find
was at a bridal shop. They had
an order for a wedding gown
of satin and lace. It had to be
all hand sewn and had to be

finished in four days. She sewed every night until three in the morning, and on the fourth night she had to sew all night. Billy was proud of his new jacket.

When Billy graduated from high school, he went off to college, never knowing how hard his mother had to work to pay his way.

After college Billy got a job and moved far away.

He had a good job as an executive with a large company. Billy was always too busy to go back home and see his mother.

Then one day his phone rang. It was a doctor from his home town. The doctor told him his mother was dying.

When Billy arrived at the
hospital, his mother was asleep.

Lying on the bed beside her was a diary which she had kept since Billy was born.

Billy had never seen the diary. He picked it up and began to read. While he waited for his mother to awaken, these are only a few of the things he read.

He noticed that after he moved away every entry in the diary was the same. "No word from Billy today, but maybe tomorrow he will come home."

As Billy closed the diary and
lay it on the bed, his mother awoke.

A smile covered her face when she saw Billy standing there.

As tears ran down Billy's cheeks, he asked, "Mama, what can I ever do to repay you for all you have done for me?"

She was very weak and unable to speak. She slowly moved her shaking hand and clutched a pencil lying on the bed.

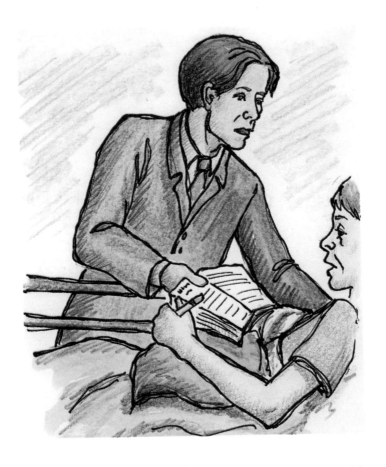

As she raised the pencil, Billy knew she wanted to write, so he opened the diary to the last page and placed it on a pillow on her chest.

With her trembling hand, she began to write. She wrote only four words before the pencil fell from her hand.

Billy picked up the diary and read, "Say you love me."

Before Billy could utter those words, she closed her eyes and fell into an eternal sleep.